SUPER SPIES

By Maria S. Barbo
Illustrated by Duendes del Sur

ABDOPUBLISHING.COM

Reinforced library bound edition published in 2017 by Spotlight, a division of ABDO. PO Box 398166, Minneapolis, Minnesota 55439. Spotlight produces high-quality reinforced library bound editions for schools and libraries. Published by agreement with Warner Bros. Entertainment Inc.

Printed in the United States of America, North Mankato, Minnesota.
042016   092016

THIS BOOK CONTAINS
RECYCLED MATERIALS

PUBLISHER'S CATALOGING IN PUBLICATION DATA

Names: Barbo, Maria S., author. | Duendes del Sur, illustrator.
Title: Scooby-Doo in super spies / by Maria S. Barbo ; illustrated by Duendes del Sur.
Description: Minneapolis, MN : Spotlight, [2017] | Series: Scooby-Doo early reading adventures
Summary: Scooby and Shaggy are playing spies. They decide to spy on Daphne and discover that she is missing! It's up to the two super spies to solve the case and find Daphne.
Identifiers: LCCN 2016930658 | ISBN 9781614794776 (lib. bdg.)
Subjects: LCSH: Scooby-Doo (Fictitious character)--Juvenile fiction. | Spies--Juvenile fiction. | Mystery and detective stories--Juvenile fiction. | Adventure and adventurers--Juvenile fiction.
Classification: DDC [Fic]--dc23
LC record available at http://lccn.loc.gov/2016930658

Spotlight

A Division of ABDO
abdopublishing.com

It was a long weekend.

Scooby and Shaggy watched too much television and played too many games.

They read all their books.

They ate all their Scooby-Snacks.

Now, Scooby is bored.

Shaggy is bored too.

Then, Shaggy has an idea.

"Let's pretend we are spies,"

says Shaggy.

Shaggy puts on a silly hat.

Scooby puts on a funny wig.

"Like, no one will know who we

are, Scoob," says Shaggy.

Shaggy picks up an old camera

that prints instant pictures.

"Look, Scoob, there is still film

in it!" says Shaggy.

Scooby and Shaggy decide to

spy on Daphne.

Shaggy sneaks over to her bed to

take a picture.

He trips and makes a loud noise.

Daphne is not in her room.

Where could she be?

Daphne is missing!

There is a mess on her bed.

Her window is open.

Her shoes are gone.

"What if a monster kidnapped Daphne?" asks Shaggy.

"Rikes!" barks Scooby.

Scooby hides under the bed.

Shaggy hides next to Scooby.

But Scooby and Shaggy must
be brave.

They are super spies.

"Look Scooby," Shaggy says.

"A ransom note!"

The super spies try reading the
handwriting, but they can't
make out what it says.

Scooby and Shaggy spy on Fred washing the Mystery Machine. Shaggy holds the camera up high to take a picture of Fred. Shaggy trips on the hose and steps in the water bucket. Water flies everywhere and splashes onto Fred.

Fred does not know where Daphne is.

Scooby and Shaggy spy on
Velma working in her room.
Scooby hears a noise.
Tick-tick-tickety-tick.
Shaggy sees books on the shelves
and wonders if they're clues. He
snaps lots of pictures while Scooby
sniffs around the room like a
master spy.
"Have you seen Daphne?" Shaggy
asks Velma.
Velma has not seen Daphne either.

Maybe Daphne is having

a snack.

Scooby and Shaggy look in

the kitchen.

A bottle of water is gone.

The bananas are missing.

"Yikes!" yells Shaggy. He trips

on a banana peel and the

camera goes flying!

"This floor sure is slippery."

Scooby and Shaggy are
good spies.
But they can't find Daphne.
Daphne is not in her bedroom.
Daphne is not with Fred.
Daphne is not with Velma.
And Daphne is not eating
in the kitchen.
Maybe a monster really did
take Daphne.
Shaggy is almost out of film.
He has one picture left.

Shaggy takes off his hat.

Scooby takes off his funny wig.

They look at all the instant

pictures they've taken.

Then, Shaggy has an idea.

Scooby hears a horn.

Shaggy sees bicycle wheels.

A monster did not kidnap Daphne.

She was riding her bike!

Daphne gives Scooby some
Scooby-Snacks.

Shaggy takes his last super
spy picture.

"Scooby-Dooby-Doo!" said Scooby.

The End